A BRAND-NEW DAY
with
MOUSE and MOLE

WONG HERBERT YEE

Green Light Readers

sandpiper

HOUGHTON MIFFLIN HARCOURT
BOSTON • NEW YORK

To Judy and Ellen
for dressing me up and down

Copyright © 2008 by Wong Herbert Yee

All rights reserved. Published in the United States by Sandpiper,
an imprint of Houghton Mifflin Harcourt Publishing Company.
Originally published in hardcover in the United States by Houghton
Mifflin Books for Children, an imprint of Houghton Mifflin
Harcourt Publishing Company, 2008.

First Green Light Readers edition 2012

SANDPIPER and the SANDPIPER logo are trademarks of
Houghton Mifflin Harcourt Publishing Company.

Green Light Readers and its logo are trademarks of
Houghton Mifflin Harcourt Publishing Company, registered in the
United States of America and/or other jurisdictions.

For information about permission to reproduce selections from this
book, write to Permissions, Houghton Mifflin Harcourt Publishing
Company, 215 Park Avenue South, New York, New York 10003.

www.hmhbooks.com

The text of this book is set in Adobe Caslon.
The illustrations are litho pencil and gouache.

Library of Congress Cataloging-in-Publication number
2007047733

ISBN: 978-0-618-96676-9 hardcover
ISBN: 978-0-547-72209-2 paperback

Manufactured in China
SCP 10 9 8 7 6 5 4

4500443034

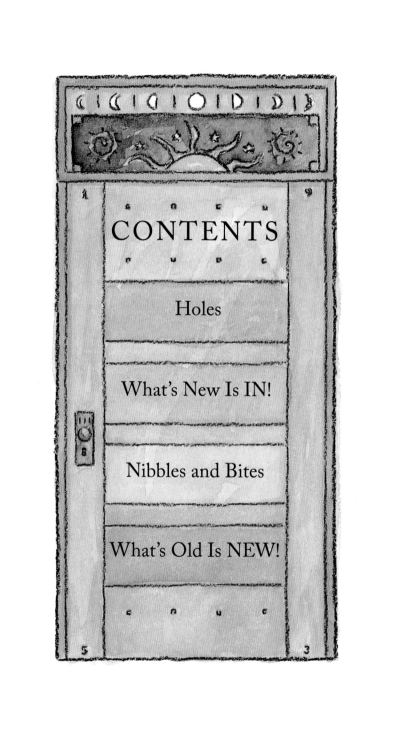

CONTENTS

HOLES

Sparrows twittered

in the oak.

It was a brand-new day!

Mole rolled out of bed.

He pulled down his shirt.

He pulled up his pants.

Mole felt a draft.

He checked the front door.
It was shut tight.
He checked the back door.
It was closed too.

"Rats!" said Mole. "There is a *hole* in
my pants!" He lifted his arm.
"Double rats!" Mole moaned.
"There is a hole in
my shirt too!"

Mole rubbed his snout. "How can I start a brand-*new* day in *old* clothes?" Luckily, Mole kept extra shirts in his dresser. He pulled the top drawer open. Several moths fluttered out.

One of Mole's shirts had a hole in the *right* elbow. Another had a hole in the *left* elbow. The third shirt had holes in both sleeves!

"Ratty-rat-rat!" muttered Mole. He yanked open the middle drawer. In it were his spare pants.

A bunch of moths flew out!

One of Mole's pants had a
hole in the *right* knee.
Another had a hole in the
left knee. The third pair
had too many holes
to count!

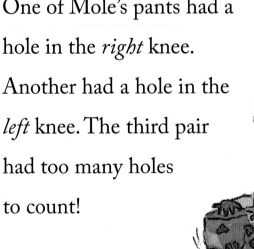

Moths put Mole in a bad mood.

TAP-TAP-TAP.

Someone was at the door.

"SCRAM!" shouted Mole.

He flung the door open.

"BEAT IT!" he hollered.

Mole waved his arms about.

"Goodness!" squeaked Mouse.

She marched upstairs in a huff.

"Wait, Mouse!" Mole cried.

"I was not talking to *you*.

It's these *pesky* moths.

Please, do come in!"

Mole raced around the room

with a broom. Mouse followed,

flapping her arms in the air.

Together, they chased

the moths out.

"Mercy, Mole!" exclaimed Mouse.

"There is a *hole* in your pants!"

Mole turned beet red. "HOLES!"

He pointed to the mound on the ground.

Mouse picked up a pair
of Mole's pants.
"Oh my!" she giggled.

The pattern of holes reminded Mouse
of Swiss cheese. Thinking of cheese
made Mouse hungry.
Her stomach grumbled.
"This is no time to think
of food!" Mole scolded.
The holes reminded *him*
of worms digging in the dirt.
Thinking of worms made *Mole* hungry.
His stomach growled.

Mole glanced at the clock.

A moth circled over his head.

Mole shooed it from the bedroom.

Mouse chased it out the door.

Huff, puff! They flopped

down on the stairs.

Mouse's stomach grumbled noisily.

"I have an idea!" she announced.

"There is a new clothing store by the diner.

Why don't we eat *first*," Mouse suggested,

"and *then* shop for new clothes?"

Mole hopped to his feet. "That sounds

like a plan!" His stomach growled

in agreement. Mouse and Mole

marched up the steps.

Mole felt a draft.

He darted back into his hole.

Mole came out with a scarf.

He tied it around his hips.

"There!" Mole nodded.

"That *hole* will be our

little secret!"

What's New Is In!

Mole handed Mouse the menu.

"I already know what I want."

Mouse smiled. "Let me guess . . .

a bowl of worms, lightly fried?"

"A *big* bowl," exclaimed Mole.

"Chasing moths is

hungry work!"

"It's a brand-new day!" declared Mouse.

"I am trying something *different.*"

Mouse flipped through the menu.

Flip-flap, flip-flap!

She could not decide what to pick.

"Oh, well!" Mouse sighed.

"Eeny, meeny, miny . . . ME!

Three-Cheese Nachos it will be."

Cheddar   Jack   Colby

After lunch, Mouse and Mole walked over to the clothes shop. Mole pressed his snout to the window. He did not see brown pants. He did not see green shirts. Green and brown were Mole's favorite colors.

He opened the door to
What's New Is IN!
"After you, Mouse,"
said Mole.

A salesclerk came up to Mouse. They both
had on the same swirly-patterned dress,
except in different colors.

"Nice outfit!" laughed the clerk.

Then she pointed to Mole.

"What's with the scarf?"

Mouse snickered. "Mole has a *big* —

Ouch!" she squeaked.

Someone was

stepping on her tail.

"Oops!" said Mouse. "What I mean is . . .
that's in case Mole gets — *too cool!*"
"*Groovy!*" The clerk nodded.

Mole looked around the store.

He looked at the clerk and cashier.

Mole looked at Mouse.

All were dressed in bright colors.

Mole's clothes were different.

Mole's clothes were drab.

He looked out of place.

Mouse held up a yellow shirt

with buttons. "This is *new!*"

Mole shook his head. "No buttons!

Buttons come loose;

buttons get lost."

Mouse picked out a purple zip top.

"This is *different!*" she hinted.

Mole shook his head. "No zippers!

Zippers are fussy;

zippers get stuck."

Mouse held plaid pants in one paw.

She held striped pants in the other.

Mole shook his head to both.

He wandered into the back room.

What's Old Is OUT! said a sign.

Mole rummaged through the racks.

"Oh, boy!" he cried. "Brown pants!"

There were green ones too.

He rummaged around some more.

"Ratty-rat-rat!" muttered Mole.

"No green or brown tops!"

Mole rubbed his snout.

It *is* a brand-new day, he thought . . .

Why not try something — *new?*

Mole picked up a shirt with fish on it.

The fish shirt had buttons.

One was missing. Mole did

not like buttons.

But he *did* like

the fish pattern.

"Fish like worms; *I* like worms!"

Mole paid the cashier.

Mouse peeked in Mole's bag.

"I thought you didn't *like* buttons?"

"It's a brand-new day!" declared Mole.

"I am trying something — *different!*"

Mouse pulled out the green pants.

"Don't you have some like this?"

"My *old* pants are brown," huffed Mole.

"Green pants are — *new!*"

Mouse shook her head.

She held the door open.

"After you, Mole!"

muttered Mouse.

Nibbles and Bites

Mole opened a box marked ACORNS.

Inside the box

was a little box

was a little box

marked HATS.

With a needle and thread,

he sewed an acorn hat to

the fish shirt.

Mole rubbed his snout. The acorn
hat was different. The acorn hat
looked out of place.
Snip, snip, snip!
Mole cut the
other buttons off.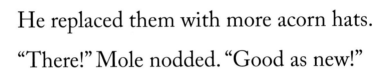
He replaced them with more acorn hats.
"There!" Mole nodded. "Good as new!"

He grabbed his fishing pole
and rushed out the door.

Mouse was on her way to the pond.

She had a fish date with Mole.

"Hey there, Mole!" Mouse waved.

Mole waved back.

"*Hay* is for horses,"

he chuckled.

Mouse stared at Mole's new fish shirt.

"Those acorn buttons are — *groovy!*"

"I'm glad you like them," said Mole.

He stuck a worm on his hook.

He popped another in his mouth.

"Fish like worms; *I* like worms!"

Mole cast his line into the water: *plop!*

Mouse took a block of
cheese from her bag.
Mouse nibbled.
Mouse gnawed.
The big block
turned into a small ball.
She stuck it on the tip of the hook.
Mouse cast her line into
the pond: *plip!*

They waited . . . and waited . . .

No nibbles. No bites.

"Want to trade places?" said Mouse.

"Whatever," yawned Mole.

He switched spots on the log
with Mouse. They waited . . .
and waited . . .

No nibbles. No bites.

Trading places did not help.

"Want to switch poles?" said Mole.

"Whatever," yawned Mouse.

She handed her pole to Mole.

Mole gave his to Mouse.

They continued to sit and wait.

No nibbles. No bites.

Switching poles did not help either.

"I have an idea!" announced Mouse.

"Why not try a *different* spot?"

Mole hopped to his feet.

"That sounds like a plan!"

Mouse and Mole climbed into the boat.

They paddled past the willow tree.

Mole cast his line into the water: *plop!*

Mouse cast her line into the pond: *plip!*

They sat and waited.

Suddenly, Mole felt a sharp tug.

"Help, Mouse!" he cried. "A BITE!"

Mole pulled and tugged on the pole.

Mouse tugged and pulled on Mole.

Snap! The line broke in two.

Mouse and Mole tumbled overboard.

Something BIG and black floated
to the surface. "A SEA MONSTER!"
hollered Mole. "Swim for your life!"
"Wait, Mole!" Mouse giggled.
"It is just an old tire."
Mole turned beet red.

"Ratty-rat-rat!" he spluttered.
Together, they rowed and
towed the tire to shore.

Mouse and Mole sat on the log
waiting for their clothes to dry.

"Boring!" yawned Mouse. She grabbed hold
of a willow vine. "YIPPEE!" she yelped.
Back and forth Mouse
swung. *Ker–SPLASH!*
Mouse jumped
into the pond.

Mole scrambled up the tree trunk.

Mole shimmied out on a branch.

"CANNONBALL!" he hollered.

SPLUNK! A plume of water
shot sky-high. Before long
their clothes were dry.
Mouse and Mole,
however, were *not!*

What's Old Is New!

Mouse rummaged through her closet.

She tossed old clothes in a box.

One dress had a stuck zipper.

Another was missing buttons.

The buttons reminded Mouse of

her neighbor downstairs.

"Only Mole would think to use

acorn tops as buttons!"

Mouse twirled her tail.
She stared at the box
of old clothes.

Tick-tock! swung the pendulum on
the clock. It reminded Mole of his
neighbor upstairs. What fun Mouse
had swinging on the vine!
Mole rubbed his snout.
He was thinking
about that old tire
at the pond.

Mouse waited for Mole to leave.

She tiptoed downstairs . . .

and into Mole's hole. Mouse took

her dress with a bad zipper.

Snip, snip, snip! Mouse cut

four patches. She sewed them

over the four elbow holes.

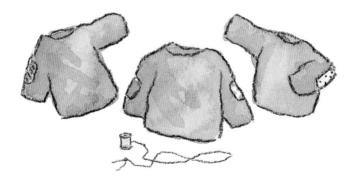

Next, it was time to mend Mole's pants.

Mouse took the top missing buttons.

Snip, snip, snip!
she cut a patch
for the right knee
on one pair and the
left knee on another.

Mouse sewed the patches in place.

"There!" She nodded. "Good as new!"

Mouse held up the third pair of pants,

the ones that looked like Swiss cheese.

Mouse could not help giggling!

Mole bought rope at the fix-it shop.

He stopped in front of **What's New Is IN!**

A mannequin wore a scarf around its hips.

TOO COOL! said the sign.

Mole rubbed his snout.

He hurried off to the pond.

Hooray! The old tire was still there.
Mole stood it upright. He gave the
tire a push. *Bumpity-bump-bump!*
It rolled all the way to the oak.

Mole peeked in Mouse's window.
Mouse was busy with flowers.

Mole got busy too.
He made a loop at one
end of the rope, then
tossed it over a branch.
Next, he fed the rope
through the loop
and pulled it snug.

Mole set the tire on a stump.
He stuck the dangling end
in the tire hole and tied
a double knot. Mole gave
the tire swing a push.
Back and forth
it swung!

Mole peeked in the box on his bed.

New patches covered *old* holes!

Mole pulled down
his *new-old* shirt.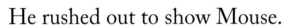
Mole pulled up
his *new-old* pants.

He rushed out to show Mouse.

TAP-TAP-TAP.

"Hey there!" huffed Mole.

Mouse giggled. "*Hay* is
for horses! I used *my* old
clothes to mend *your*
old clothes. I hope
you like them!"

"The patches are *new;* the patches are
different. The patches are — *too COOL!*"
Mole chuckled. "I have fixed
something old as well."
Mole covered Mouse's
eyes with a scarf.

He led Mouse down the steps.
"ABRACADABRA!" shouted Mole.
He yanked the scarf off.
Mouse rubbed her eyes in wonder.
"Only you, Mole, would think
to use an *old* tire for
a NEW swing!"

Mouse scrambled up
in the tire swing.
Mole gave her
a *little* push.

"Higher!" Mouse squeaked.
Mole gave the tire swing a BIG push.
"YIPPEE!" yelped Mouse.
Then it was Mole's turn. Back and
forth they swung, until moths came
out to play. They chased Mouse
inside her house and Mole
down into his hole.